# Stars of the Show

**Heather Hammonds**

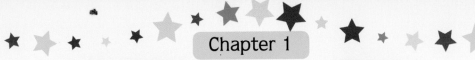

# Putting on a Play

Have you ever been to a play?
A play is a kind of story.

The story is told by **actors** on a **stage**.

Maya's class is putting on a play.
Their teacher is helping them.

# Writing the Play

Maya's class is writing their own play. Everyone makes up part of the story.

The teacher writes the play on some paper. This is called a play **script**.

The Dog Who Wanted to Fly

There are people and animals in the play.
The play is about a dog who wants to fly!

## The Dog Who Wanted to Fly

*Digger the dog is running about in the garden.*

**Digger:** Birds can fly.
If I wave my paws,
maybe I can fly too!

*Chirpy the bird flies into the garden.*

**Chirpy:** Digger,
what are you doing?
Dogs can't fly!

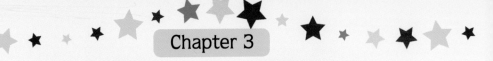

## Chapter 3

# A Team of Helpers

Everyone in Maya's class helps put on the play.

Some children will be the actors.
They will be the people and animals
in the play.

Mrs Johnson, Digger's Owner

Digger, the Dog

Chirpy, the Bird

Mr Johnson, Digger's Owner

Some children will look after the lights.
They will shine the lights on to the stage.

Some children will make sounds in the play.
They will make lots of special noises.

Some children will make the **costumes**.
Mums and dads will help them.

Some children will build the **set**.
Mums and dads will help them too.

The teacher will help everyone!

Things To Do:
· Sort Costumes
· Lighting

9

## Chapter 4

# Learning Lines

The words in a play script are called **lines**. Actors must remember their lines when they are in a play.

Mr and Mrs Johnson walk into the garden.

*Chirpy the bird is flying around.*

*Digger the dog is trying to copy Chirpy.*

**Mrs Johnson:**

What is Digger doing?

**Mr Johnson:**

I think he is trying to fly.

He is copying that bird.

**Mrs Johnson:**

Silly Digger.

He is a dog, not a bird!

Maya is going to be Mrs Johnson in the play.
She learns her lines.
The other actors learn their lines too.

## Chapter 5

# Working Hard

Putting on a play is hard work.
The lights and sounds are almost ready.
The costumes are almost ready.
The set is almost ready too.

Maya and her friends make a poster
about the play.
The teacher puts the poster up.

# COME TO OUR PLAY!

## Friday night at 7 o'clock.

## Grade Two classroom

## All welcome

## Chapter 6

# The Big Night

On the night of the play,
the actors put on their costumes.
They put on **make-up** too.

The **audience** sits in front of the stage.
They wait for the play to begin.

Mums and dads help out **backstage.**
The teacher checks that everyone is ready.

Paula and Asha turn on the lights.
Kelvin and Raj play some music.
The play begins.

## Chapter 7

# Show Time!

Tony is Digger the dog.
He runs about on the stage.
The audience laughs when he tries to fly.

The other actors take their turn
on the stage too.
Everyone remembers their lines.

The audience claps and cheers
when the play is over.
The actors **bow** to the audience.
They are the stars of the show!

The teacher takes some photos of the children.
Mums and dads take some photos too.

## Chapter 8

# After the Play

After the play, there is a party. Everyone who helped with the play goes to the party.

The class thanks the teacher
for helping them with the play.
They thank the mums and dads
for helping them too.

Putting on a play was lots of fun!

# Glossary

**actors** — people who act out a story in a play

**audience** — the people who watch a play

**backstage** — a place behind the stage where actors and those working in a play go

**bow** — to bend from the waist, as a way of saying thank you

**costumes** — special clothes made for a play

**lines** — the words actors say in a play

**make-up** — special paints put on an actor's face

**script** — the words or story in a play

**set** — the part of a stage that is built to look like a place in a play

**stage** — a place (usually inside a building) where a play is held

# Index